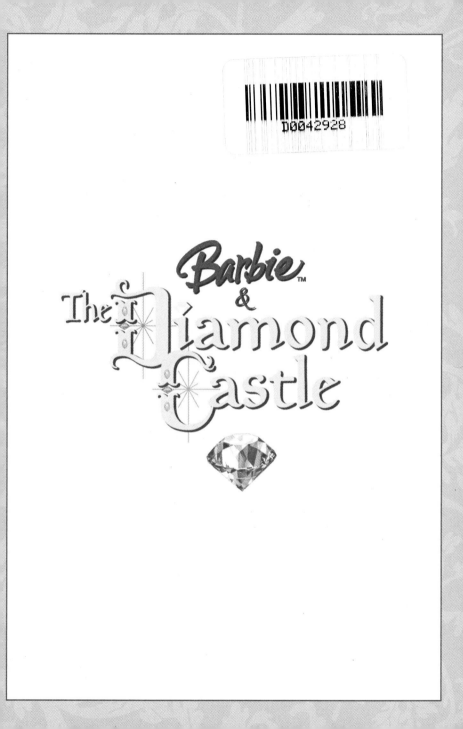

Barbie™
&
The Diamond
Castle

A Junior Novelization

Adapted by Shannon Penney
Based on the original screenplay
by Cliff Ruby & Elana Lesser
Illustrations by Ulkutay Design Group
and Allan Choi

SCHOLASTIC INC.

New York   Toronto   London   Auckland   Sydney
Mexico City   New Delhi   Hong Kong   Buenos Aires

ISBN-13: 978-0-545-08120-7
ISBN-10: 0-545-08120-3

BARBIE and associated trademarks and trade dress are
owned by, and used under license from, Mattel, Inc.
© 2008 Mattel, Inc. All Rights Reserved.
"Believe" written by Amy Powers, Russell De Salvo, and Rob Hudnut.
© 2007 Mattel, Inc. All Rights Reserved.

Special Thanks to Rob Hudnut, Shelley Dvi-Vardhana, Vicki Jaeger,
Monica Okazaki, Christine Chang, Jennifer Twiner McCarron,
Shawn McCorkindale, Pat Link, Tulin Ulkutay, and Ayse Ulkutay.

Published by Scholastic Inc.
SCHOLASTIC and associated logos are trademarks and/or
registered trademarks of Scholastic Inc.

12 11 10 9 8 7 6 5 4 3 2   8 9 10 11 12/0

Printed in the U.S.A.
First printing, September 2008

Introduction

Light streamed through the window as Barbie sat on the end of her bed, humming and strumming her guitar. Her best friend, Teresa, joined in. The girls were writing a song!

SLAM! Barbie's little sister, Stacie, stormed through the door.

"I never want to see her again!" she fumed. "She's SO not my friend anymore."

Teresa looked shocked, but Barbie could guess what had happened. "Did you

1

have a fight with Courtney?" she asked sympathetically.

"You mean, the backstabber?" Stacie snapped, flopping down on the bed. "What's the point of even having friends? They just turn on you."

Barbie put an arm around her sister's shoulders. "Not *real* friends. Real friends care, even if you make a mistake."

Stacie narrowed her eyes. "I think they just let you down when it counts."

"You're not the only person to think that," Barbie said slowly. "I know a story about best friends who thought that, too. They lived in a world with good and bad magic, flying serpents, a Diamond Castle. . . ."

Stacie couldn't help being interested. "What happened?"

"One day, they had a terrible fight," Barbie said. She strummed her guitar, and Stacie inched closer. "It all started with music. They loved to sing together, just like me and Teresa. . . ."

Chapter 1

Liana and Alexa were the very best of friends. They lived together in a tiny cottage surrounded by hundreds of blooming flowers. The girls lovingly cared for their garden, making sure all the flowers got plenty of water and sunshine. When the flowers were in full bloom, Liana and Alexa sold them at the village nearby. It was a simple life, but the two best friends were very happy with what they had: their music and their friendship.

One evening, the two girls settled down by the fire inside their cottage. They pulled out their guitars, strumming and singing together.

"That song sounds magical," Alexa noted.

Liana laughed. "Everything sounds magical to you, Alexa!"

"That's because I believe in magic. And wishes . . ."

"And dreams that come true?" Liana added.

Alexa smiled. "Always!"

"Good," Liana said, giggling and tossing a dishcloth to her friend. "Then it's your night to do the dishes. That's *my* dream come true!"

❀ ❀ ❀

The next day, the two best friends headed out to the garden again. There were so many flowers to pick!

Before long, Alexa heard Liana calling from the nearby stream. Liana had stepped across the water on some stones. "Come here! I'll help you," she said.

Alexa wasn't so sure. Golden-haired

Liana was the more adventurous of the two friends. But Alexa cautiously followed her friend into the middle of the stream. Once they had reached the right spot, Liana pointed into the water.

Just below the surface were two identical heart-shaped stones, glistening in the sunlight. Liana pulled them out.

Alexa gasped. "They're beautiful! They almost look —"

"— magical?" Liana finished. "I think so, too. And look, there's one for each of us."

"What if we make them into necklaces?" Alexa suggested.

The girls grinned widely at each other, holding the beautiful stones in their hands. "Best friends today . . ." Alexa began.

". . . tomorrow . . ." Liana added.

". . . and always!" they finished together.

For a brief second, the stones twinkled in their hands. Liana and Alexa didn't notice, because just then, a strong gust of wind blew through the garden. The two friends looked up to see dark clouds roll in front of the sun. The wind howled, thunder clapped, and lightning cracked. Before long, a heavy rain poured down from the sky. Liana and Alexa ran for cover.

Inside the cottage, Liana added woven chains to the two heart-shaped stones while the girls waited out the storm. The necklaces she made matched perfectly!

When the storm finally ended and sun trickled in through the window, Liana and Alexa slowly opened the front door. They couldn't believe their eyes. Uprooted flowers were strewn everywhere. Fallen tree branches littered the ground. Their garden was completely destroyed!

The friends gathered what flowers they could and brought them inside.

Alexa sighed sadly. "Even if we sell all of these, the money will never last us until next season."

Liana put on a brave face. "Of course it will. Now, what would you like for lunch? We have bread and jam . . . or jam and bread." She began to make a sandwich.

"You know what I would wish for if these stones were really magic?" Alexa asked, touching her necklace. "More food than we could possibly eat, more house than we could ever explore, more clothes than we could ever wear. Then we'd never have to worry about another thing ever again!"

Liana rolled her eyes. "Except how spoiled we'd be!"

In spite of everything, Alexa couldn't help laughing, too.

Chapter 2

Liana and Alexa carried some flowers into town later that afternoon, joking and laughing to keep their spirits up. But when they passed a little old woman along the side of the road, shivering in a tattered cloak, their laughter stopped.

Liana walked up to the woman, holding out her jam sandwich. "May I share this with you?" she asked kindly.

The woman took a big bite of the sandwich. "Please let me repay you," she

said. "Take one of my treasures." She gestured to a strange collection of things around her feet: scraps of cloth, a broken comb, a tarnished hand mirror, an old boot.

"I couldn't," Liana said. The old woman's face fell.

"You don't want to hurt her feelings," Alexa whispered to her friend.

Liana reached down for the hand mirror. "Well . . . maybe this?"

The woman nodded. "A nice present for a nice girl."

Liana thanked the woman, and the girls continued on, not noticing that the mirror twinkled for a moment . . . almost like magic.

Later that afternoon, Liana and Alexa returned to their cottage. Alexa counted the money they had made. It wasn't much.

Liana, meanwhile, was busy polishing the little hand mirror. When she was through, the gold frame sparkled.

Alexa couldn't believe her eyes. "Now *that* is magical."

"That poor old woman didn't realize what she had," Liana said. She carefully tucked the mirror into her basket and headed outside.

The girls spent the rest of the day picking up branches and cleaning up the devastated garden. They sang together as they worked. But soon a third voice had joined them — and it was coming from Liana's basket!

Liana reached into her basket and pulled out the hand mirror. The face of a girl with long golden hair looked back at them. She was happily singing along! As soon as she spotted Liana and Alexa, she stopped abruptly.

"I couldn't resist," she said apologetically. "I'll stop if it bothers you."

Alexa's eyes grew wider and wider. "Are you . . . real?"

The girl suddenly looked worried. "I'm nobody. Just pretend you never saw me." With that, she disappeared.

"Wait — don't go!" Liana cried. She and Alexa looked at each other and began to sing again.

Before long, the girl in the mirror joined them!

"Please don't disappear," Liana pleaded after they'd finished their song. "Can you tell us your name?"

"It's Melody," the girl said hesitantly.

Alexa spoke up, nervous. "I don't mean to be rude, but are you the enchanted spirit of the mirror? Was the old woman who gave it to us a sorceress?"

Melody giggled. "No, she was just an old woman, and I'm just . . ." She trailed off, her face falling. "I'm sorry. I shouldn't be telling you any of this. It's incredibly dangerous for you."

Liana and Alexa exchanged a glance. "Dangerous?"

Chapter 3

Not far from Liana and Alexa's cottage, there was a dark cave cut into the side of a mountain. It was huge and echoing, lit within by flaming torches. A moat of hissing lava ran around the floor inside.

This was Lydia's home.

Lydia was an evil sorceress. She lived in the cave with her giant winged serpent, Slyder. Slyder did Lydia's bidding, no matter how dark or wicked.

On this day, Slyder slithered through the
cave to find Lydia. He bowed and hissed,
"Mistressssss, I can senssssse her sssssinging,
ssssomewhere wesssst." He had heard
Melody singing! Lydia had been searching
for Melody for a long time.

Lydia smiled cruelly, circling the marble

statues of Dori and Phedra, two of the muses of music. "Bring her to me," she instructed the serpent.

Slyder bowed and slithered away.

Chapter 4

The next morning, Liana and Alexa tidied up the cottage while Melody sang to them. Liana and Alexa convinced her to teach them her beautiful song. They were fast learners, and soon the three girls were singing together in harmony.

But they didn't know that they had an audience.

Slyder, circling overhead, had followed Melody's voice to the cottage. His shadow fell across the ground, and Liana rushed to the window, holding up Melody's mirror. The serpent swooped closer, in search of the muse apprentice, and saw Melody in the mirror.

"Slyder!" Melody cried. "We have to hide — *now!*"

"The cellar. Go!" Liana called, handing the mirror to Alexa. "I'll be right there."

As Alexa ran downstairs with Melody,

Liana grabbed an old wooden hand mirror from her dresser, hurriedly tucked it under her mattress, and followed her friends to the cellar.

Not a moment too soon.

Slyder slammed into the front door of the cottage with his huge head, knocking the door off its hinges. His tongue flicked as he searched the room, sliding across the wooden floors. He spotted something sticking out from under Liana's mattress. The hand mirror!

As Slyder searched the cottage, Liana, Alexa, and Melody snuck outside through the cellar. They raced across the garden and into the nearby forest just as Slyder emerged. He bumped his head on the low door and screamed. The whole cottage shook.

Walls cracked. Windows shattered. Curtains fell and landed near the roaring fireplace.

As the cottage caught on fire and smoke curled from the windows, Slyder smiled wickedly. Wooden mirror in hand, he took to the sky and flew back to his mistress.

When he reached the cave, Slyder proudly presented the mirror to Lydia. "I sssaw Melody in thisss mirror," Slyder explained. "It wasss held by a light-haired girl, who wasss with her dark-haired friend."

"Then they tricked you," Lydia hissed. "There's no magic in this mirror!"

"I took it from their cottage myssself!" Slyder cried.

She shattered the mirror against a stone pillar. "Once again, I have to do everything myself!"

Chapter 5

Once Slyder disappeared, Liana and Alexa rushed out of the woods, holding Melody's mirror. The cottage had burned to the ground.

"There's nothing left," Alexa said in shock.

"This is all my fault," Melody said sadly. "Throw me far away before he comes back."

Liana studied Melody's pained face. "What does he want with you?"

"It's his mistress, Lydia," Melody said.

"She knows that I have the key to the Diamond Castle."

"The Diamond Castle?" Liana repeated.

"It's my home," Melody explained. "The birthplace of music. Every time a new song is sung anywhere in the world, a diamond appears on the castle walls."

Liana and Alexa listened carefully as Melody went on.

"I lived there with Dori, Phedra, and Lydia — the three Muses of Music. They took care of the Diamond Castle, and I was their apprentice. They were friends, but Lydia wanted to be the one and only muse."

"What happened?" Liana asked.

Melody sighed. "Lydia found an ancient cave filled with magic and transformed her flute into an instrument of darkness." Melody shuddered at the memory. "With

her new powers, she planned to take over. The other muses hid their instruments and the castle, and gave me the key in case anything happened to them. Lydia turned them to marble."

Liana and Alexa gasped.

"I ran and ran," Melody continued.

"Slyder was chasing me. And then I saw my only chance. I hid in the old woman's hand mirror. Slyder broke my magic whistle, trapping me in the mirror. I was so afraid, I never said a word . . . until I met you two. And now I've ruined everything. Slyder heard me singing and followed me here."

Liana looked thoughtful. "But if you have the key, do you know where the Diamond Castle is hidden?"

"Yes." Melody nodded. "It's in a glade, far to the west."

"What about Lydia?" Liana asked. "Can you stop her?"

"I think if I play the muses' instruments, I can break her spell," Melody replied.

Alexa shook her head. She knew what her friend was thinking. "Liana, we're talking about dark muses and serpents and real magic here."

Liana raised her eyebrows. "You love magic!"

"I love *good* magic," Alexa corrected her friend.

"Melody, what happens if Lydia destroys the muses' instruments?" Liana asked.

"She wins," Melody replied. "Our world will be nothing but shadows and sorrow."

Alexa glanced at what was left of the cottage and frowned. "Kind of like our home."

"Lydia and Slyder did that to us," Liana pointed out. "We can't let that and worse happen to other people, can we?"

Alexa thought about it for a moment. Then she smiled — she was in.

"Are you really going to help me fight Lydia?" Melody asked the girls.

Alexa nodded. "It's the three of us now, Melody. Just do me a favor. I love your voice, but *please* don't sing."

With that, Liana and Alexa turned and walked away from their charred cottage, Melody's mirror in hand.

Chapter 6

The three friends had a long way to go in search of the Diamond Castle. Melody said that once they found the Seven Stones, they'd be close. Liana and Alexa walked along forest trails, over hills, and camped under the stars.

The next morning, Liana called out excitedly at the crest of one hill, then scrambled back down to help Alexa to the top. Below them were beautiful flowers as far as the eye could see.

Melody cheered. "We made it to the Valley of Flowers!"

Liana led the way through the valley, stopping now and then to smell a rose or a lily.

After a few minutes, Alexa whispered, "I think we're being followed." She turned and pointed to a hollow log moving along the ground.

Liana stepped up bravely to investigate, with Alexa close behind. Alexa saw something inside the log move, and she yelped. But Liana giggled, bent down, and stood up with a little cocker spaniel puppy in her arms! Then a white Westie puppy jumped into Alexa's arms, tail wagging happily.

Liana hugged the cocker spaniel. "Where did they come from? There's nobody for miles."

"They must be lost," Alexa said.

Liana held the cocker spaniel in one hand and the mirror in the other. "What do you think, Melody?"

"Look at those sparkly little eyes!" Melody said, admiring the puppy.

Liana smiled. "I like that. I hereby name you Sparkles," she said to the cocker spaniel.

"And your name is Lily, like the beautiful flower," Alexa said, stroking the Westie's ears.

"They must be starving!" Liana noted.

Alexa groaned. "Don't even talk about food. My stomach has been rumbling for miles."

"So *that's* what I was hearing," Melody teased as the friends walked on through the valley. "I thought it was thunder. . . ."

"Or stampeding horses," Liana added.

"Or bellowing bullfrogs!" Melody cried.

Alexa rolled her eyes.

"Or jump-roping elephants," Liana added, after a long pause. She and Melody dissolved into giggles, and Alexa couldn't help joining in.

Later that day, the girls finally came to a small village. They were hungry and exhausted, and could smell the delicious food at the local inn. But they didn't have any money. All they could do was look hungrily through the inn windows.

Suddenly, the innkeeper stormed outside and whirled to face the girls. "Have you seen them?" he asked gruffly. "Those good-for-nothing musicians were due here an hour ago. People are getting restless!"

Shouts came from inside. "Where's the music? Bring on the singers!"

"Hold your horses, they're coming!" the innkeeper bellowed back.

"Actually, they're here!" Liana said, her face lighting up. "We're the substitute musicians. We're very good, and we'll only cost you —"

"A meal!" Alexa jumped in, catching on to Liana's plan. "I mean, two meals. And two doggie bags," she added, gesturing to the puppies.

Before they knew it, Liana and Alexa had been ushered inside to the stage. They chose two guitars and turned to the rowdy audience, smiling. The two girls began to play, while Melody hummed along from the side of the stage. It wasn't long before the crowd settled down.

After a few songs — and a lot of applause — the innkeeper brought two plates of food up to Liana and Alexa. The girls jumped down from the stage, mouths watering, and sat at an empty table.

Two young men — twins — sauntered up

to the table. They both carried guitars.
These were the missing musicians! "Mind
if we join you?" one asked.

"You owe us," the other teased.

"We don't even know you," Alexa
responded, raising her eyebrows.

"And yet you took our gig," one twin said, shaking his head jokingly.

Liana laughed. "A gig you lost when you failed to show up! But the seats are yours."

The twins sat down and introduced themselves as Jeremy and Ian. They began strumming their guitars, singing a silly song they made up on the spot. After Liana and Alexa finished eating, it was time for them to go. Alexa didn't realize it, but as she walked away, she dropped her handkerchief.

After the girls had left, Ian plucked Alexa's handkerchief from the floor.

"I'm guessing they left it on purpose," Jeremy said, grinning. "The only polite thing to do is find them."

❀ ❀ ❀

Only a few minutes after the girls had left the inn with Sparkles, Lily, and Melody, a dark shadow swooped across the sky. Slyder landed in the village plaza, and Lydia climbed down from his back. She nodded toward the inn. "If they've been here, someone there will know something."

Lydia entered the inn and approached the innkeeper. "I'm looking for two girls," she said. "One light-haired, one dark-haired. Did they pass this way?"

"I — I don't remember," the innkeeper stammered.

Lydia glared at him. "Oh, really?" She pulled the magic flute from her pocket and began to play. The innkeeper and his patrons all fell under her spell.

"Let's try again," Lydia whispered. "Where are the girls?"

"Out back, down the trail," the mesmerized innkeeper said.

Lydia cackled gleefully and stormed into the dark night.

Chapter 7

Liana and Alexa walked quickly along the edge of the dark forest outside town, carrying Sparkles, Lily, and Melody. They had only the moonlight to guide them.

They didn't realize that they were being followed.

Slyder swooped down from the sky, blocking their path. They turned to run the other way, only to find Lydia standing there.

"Lydia!" Alexa gasped.

"So you know my name," Lydia said softly. "I wonder who could have told you?"

Alexa's eyes widened in horror. Lydia knew that Melody was with them!

"Give me the mirror," Lydia demanded.

Liana gathered her courage and stepped forward. "We won't."

Lydia reached inside her robes. "I'll have to do things my way." She pulled out her flute and began to play.

A magical flash flickered between Liana's and Alexa's stone necklaces, but they didn't see it.

"Give me the mirror. *Now*," Lydia said.

Liana glanced at Alexa. "Never!" she cried. "Run, Alexa!"

They weren't under Lydia's spell!

Liana and Alexa ran deep into the shadowy forest, finally ducking inside a hollow tree. Sparkles and Lily peeked out of their baskets, whimpering. They could all hear Slyder nearby, searching for them.

The serpent slithered closer and closer to the tree. He reared back, ready to attack, but the two friends bolted out of the tree — just in time!

Slyder turned and gave chase, nipping at the girls' heels. Just as he was about to overtake them, two horses galloped through the trees. Jeremy swept Liana onto his horse, while Ian pulled Alexa onto his.

The horses barreled through the forest, dodging branches and tree roots. Slyder flew after them, his yellow eyes glowing in the darkness.

Alexa and Liana gasped as Slyder suddenly swooped down in front of them, blocking the path!

Ian and Jeremy steered their horses quickly around either side of the serpent. Slyder was right behind them now . . . but Jeremy rode through a curtain of ivy into a tunnel, with Ian and Alexa close behind. Ian pulled the ivy down after him. Rocks and dirt slid from above, blocking the tunnel's entrance.

Slyder slammed his head into the rocks, trying to break through. After a large rock fell on his head, he was too dizzy to keep trying. He turned and stumbled back to Lydia, mumbling excuses.

Inside the tunnel, Jeremy and Ian helped the girls down from the horses.

Ian pulled Alexa's handkerchief out of his pocket with a flourish.

"Thank you," Alexa said. "That's very thoughtful . . . for a rascal."

The twins laughed. "So, we know you're being chased by a giant winged serpent-beast. Anything else we should know?" Jeremy asked.

Liana and Alexa looked at each other knowingly.

"Not really . . ." Alexa said.

"Except that a very dear friend of ours is a muse who's trapped inside a mirror," Liana added.

Jeremy and Ian burst out laughing.

Liana pulled the mirror out of her basket and turned to Melody.

The twins stared at Melody, stunned and speechless.

"How did you escape Lydia's music?" Melody asked.

The girls shook their heads. "Luck?" Alexa guessed.

Jeremy cleared his throat. "I have a feeling I'm going to regret asking, but . . . is there anything else we should know?"

Chapter 8

The next morning, the twins led the way out the far end of the tunnel on horseback. Up ahead, they could all see a broad river, sparkling in the morning sunlight.

Liana held up Melody's mirror. "This is good," Melody said. "We just have to make it across the river to the Seven Stones."

"Ian, do you remember those odd rocks we passed last spring, near here?" Jeremy asked.

Ian nodded. "There was something almost magical about them."

An image of the Seven Stones appeared in Melody's mirror, and Jeremy grinned. "Same place," he said. "I know exactly where it is."

The group rode along the trail until they reached a fork. One path led down to the river. A sign marked BRIDGE pointed the way. But Jeremy and Ian steered the horses down the other path.

"Wait!" Liana cried. "The sign shows a bridge that way."

"Probably washed out long ago," Jeremy said casually.

Sparkles and Lily leaped out of their baskets and ran off down the bridge path, yelping cheerfully.

"Sparkles!" Liana cried. She and Alexa jumped down from the horses and followed the puppies.

When they reached the river's edge, the girls could hear the puppies whimpering, but they couldn't see them. "Something's wrong," Alexa whispered.

And something was — a squat, hairy troll leaped out from behind a nearby boulder! He held one puppy in each hand. "Looking for these morsels?" he mumbled gruffly.

"Put them down!" Liana cried.

"Why would I do that?" the troll scoffed.

Jeremy's voice rang through the air. "Common courtesy?"

The troll spun around to see the twins approaching on horseback. He scowled. "I know you. Double Trouble! You owe me!"

Jeremy and Ian pulled daggers from

their belts, and the troll let go of Sparkles and Lily. Then he reached behind him and produced a giant sword!

"He's got a point," Jeremy said under his breath, glancing at his brother.

Ian raised his eyebrows. "Yes, a rather sharp one."

Rather than attacking the twins with the sword, the troll plunged it into the ground and pulled on it like a lever. The ground beneath Jeremy and Ian gave way, and they fell into a deep pit!

The troll smiled triumphantly.

Liana stepped forward. "Thank you for releasing the dogs. You'll free the gentlemen next," she demanded.

The troll snickered. "Free 'em? I'm going to *eat* 'em! They owe me their lives. They wanted to cross my bridge."

Liana looked out across the open river. "But there isn't any bridge."

"'Course there is," said the troll. "*If* you answer my riddle. They failed, just like everybody else."

Liana glanced at Alexa, then down at the pit. She took a deep breath. "Then ask *us* your riddle. If we answer correctly, you let them go. If we don't, you have dinner for tomorrow night, too."

Alexa couldn't believe what she was hearing. "*Dinner?* What are you doing?!" she whispered to her friend.

The troll grinned from ear to ear. "It's a deal! Nobody's ever answered my riddle correctly. Ready? What instrument can you hear but can't see and can't touch?"

Liana and Alexa looked at each other

blankly. "It's a trick," Alexa whispered. "There's no instrument like that."

Liana reached into her basket and pulled out the mirror. "Melody, what do you think?"

"I don't know," Melody said, thinking hard. "You play every instrument I know with your hands or your mouth."

"*Ding!*" the troll cried. "Time's up!"

"Good," Liana responded evenly. "Because I have the answer: your voice. You can't see it or touch it, but when you sing, everybody can hear it."

The troll's eyes bulged. His jaw dropped. He stomped his foot.

Liana was right!

Behind the troll, a magical bridge slowly appeared, stretching across the water.

Sparkles and Lily scampered to the bridge, barking. Liana and Alexa followed cautiously. As soon as the girls' feet touched the bridge, they were magically swept across the water with the puppies.

The troll was still stomping along the riverbank, working himself into a fury. Before long, he disappeared in a puff of smoke . . . just as Jeremy and Ian pulled themselves out of the pit.

"Bad day for him," Ian noted.

The twins moved to step onto the end of the bridge, but as they did, it began to vanish.

"Hey, girls! Wait for us!" Jeremy called.

The girls had been swept almost to the other side of the river. There was no turning back. "We can't!" Alexa cried.

Liana's voice chimed in. "Meet us at the Seven Stones!"

With that, they disappeared from sight.

"What's wrong with this picture?" Jeremy asked, looking at the spot where the bridge had been only seconds before.

Ian smiled wryly. "Everything," he responded.

Chapter 9

Hours later, Liana, Alexa, Melody, and the puppies were still searching for the Seven Stones. Alexa plopped down on the ground. "Do we have any water?"

"We ran out," Liana said. "About an hour after we ran out of food."

Even the puppies looked disappointed.

A light glistening through the trees ahead caught Liana's eye. "I see something!" she cried.

Alexa, Sparkles, and Lily all jumped to

their feet and followed Liana down the path. Before long, they had reached a beautiful manor surrounded by flower gardens. The windows were lit with a warm glow.

Alexa looked around in awe, knocking on the front door. "I wonder if someone royal lives here?"

A butler and a maid answered the door promptly. The butler bowed. "Ah, you've come at last!"

Liana and Alexa glanced at each other, confused. But before they could ask any questions, Sparkles barked happily and scurried into the house. Liana followed the frisky puppy, with Alexa and Lily on her heels.

When they caught up with Sparkles, the girls couldn't believe their eyes. She had led them to a huge table filled with food!

"There's enough for an army," Alexa gasped.

The butler and maid entered the room. "M'ladies, this is all yours. The grounds, the house, everything. It all belongs to you," the butler said.

Liana's eyes nearly popped out of her head. "But that's impossible!" she said.

"The legend," the butler stated simply. "It's been foretold that two best friends, one light-haired and one dark-haired, will come to live in the house. Only then are we free to leave."

"You've arrived, just as the legend foretold," the maid added. "So if it pleases you, may we leave?"

Without waiting for an answer, the butler and maid turned to go, handing Liana the keys on their way out.

The two friends looked at each other, dumbstruck. Liana pulled Melody's mirror from her basket. "What do you think, Melody?"

Melody studied the ornate room. "You know, the muses sing songs about legends and destiny. This really could be yours."

Alexa couldn't take her eyes off the grand table. "So if it's ours . . . do you think we can eat something?" she asked. The girls dove in, piling plates with delicious food for themselves and the puppies.

As she ate, Alexa explored the room, pulling open the doors of a huge armoire. It was packed with incredible dresses!

"They're beautiful," Liana breathed.

"And just our sizes!" Alexa added. "How's that for destiny?" She pulled out a dress, held it in front of her, and admired her reflection in a nearby mirror. "Liana, do you realize? It's exactly what I dreamed of. More food than we could possibly eat, more house than we could ever explore, more clothes than we could ever wear. No worries ever again."

Liana raised her eyebrows. "Right, except for Lydia, and Slyder, and the future of the world if we don't get Melody to the Diamond Castle."

Alexa was silent for a moment. Then she said quietly, "I just don't see why we should risk our lives, when we suddenly have everything we ever wanted."

"We promised Melody we'd help," Liana reminded her. "Friends stick together."

"Sure, when it's for something you want," Alexa replied. "You always want adventure and excitement, and I always come along because I'm your friend. This time, I want something. If friends stick together, stay here with me."

Liana's face fell. "I can't do that."

"Well, I can't go," Alexa said simply.

There was a long pause. Sparkles watched the girls anxiously, while Lily hid her eyes behind her paws.

Finally, Liana cleared her throat. "Then I guess this is good-bye," she said. She

picked up Melody's mirror in one hand and scooped up Sparkles in the other. "Let's go, Melody."

"This makes no sense!" Melody cried. "Think about what you're doing! You're best friends!" Liana tucked the mirror in her basket and walked out the door.

Alexa yanked off her heart-shaped necklace and tossed it on the floor. Lily whimpered and slipped it over her own neck for safekeeping.

Just then, there was a noise at the back door. Alexa looked up hopefully, brightening. "Liana?" she called, running to the door. But when she pulled it open, a dark shadow fell over her.

Slyder.

Before Alexa knew what was happening, the giant serpent had scooped her up with his tail. He quickly flew Alexa and Lily to Lydia's cave.

Lydia was thrilled to see them. "Liked the manor, did you?" she asked Alexa knowingly. "So terribly . . . tempting?"

Alexa gasped. "This was all your doing! The servants were under your power!"

Lydia chuckled. "Just my little way of getting you here for a visit," she said. "Now, give me the mirror."

"I don't have it," Alexa said, trembling.

Slyder poked his head into Alexa's basket, searching. "No mirror, missssstressss," he reported.

"So the other girl has it," Lydia murmured. She spun to face Alexa. "Where is your friend? Or should I say, ex-friend?"

"I — I don't know," Alexa said.

Lydia pulled out her flute and put it to her lips.

Alexa frowned. "That doesn't work on me."

"Bold words for a girl who no longer wears her necklace," Lydia cackled. "As long as you and your friend were loyal to each other, the stones protected you. But now . . ."

The evil muse began to play her flute, and within seconds, Alexa had fallen under her spell.

"Where is she?" Lydia repeated.

Alexa's eyes glazed over. "Going to the Seven Stones," she said flatly.

Lydia turned to Slyder. "Get the girl and the mirror," she ordered. "And this time, do it right."

Slyder bowed and slithered into the dark night.

Chapter 10

Melody's voice carried gleefully through the darkness. "The Seven Stones! We're here!"

Liana couldn't help cheering. They'd finally arrived!

"Just down there is the misty glade and the Diamond Castle," Melody continued. She paused sadly. "I wish Alexa were with us. I know you miss her."

Liana hung her head. "I don't just miss her . . . I feel like a part of me is gone."

Lost in thought, she didn't notice when Sparkles began barking.

"What is it, girl?" Melody asked the puppy.

They found out too soon, as Slyder swooped down from the sky. He seized Liana and flew back to Lydia's cave, leaving Sparkles behind.

"Welcome, darling," Lydia greeted Liana, tying her securely to a column. Alexa appeared at Lydia's side, mesmerized. "She told me where to find you," Lydia explained. "Friends always turn on you, sooner or later." With that, she reached into Liana's basket and pulled out the hand mirror.

"Melody," she called, peering into the glass. "Come out now." But the mirror showed only Lydia's own reflection. "Stubborn girl," Lydia hissed. She ordered Alexa to walk toward the blazing, hissing lava pit that ran around the edge of the cave.

Liana struggled frantically. "No! Alexa, stop!"

"She only listens to me," Lydia said calmly. "And I'll only stop her if Melody

asks me to." She peered into the glass as
Alexa moved closer and closer to the edge
of the pit.

Suddenly, Melody's face appeared in the
mirror. "Stop her, Lydia."

Lydia cackled with delight. "So nice to
see you again! Take me to the Diamond
Castle."

"Stop her, and I will," Melody reluctantly promised.

Lydia called out to Alexa, who stopped only half a step from the edge of the lava. Then the wicked muse turned back to Melody. "Show me where the castle is, and then I'll release your friends." Lydia carried Melody's mirror out into the night. "Meet me outside, Slyder," she said, glancing back at the serpent meaningfully.

Slyder knew what his mistress wanted him to do. He slithered over to Liana and bit through the ropes that bound her.

Without hesitating, Liana ran to Alexa's side. "Alexa, wake up!"

Neither girl noticed Slyder creeping up behind them. With a flick of his tail, he knocked Liana and Alexa over the side of the lava pit! Then he left the cave.

Lily ran to the edge and peered into the lava pit, whimpering.

Fortunately, Liana and Alexa had landed on an outcropping near the ledge. Liana sat up carefully and looked around.

Alexa was near her, but still under Lydia's evil spell!

"I'm so sorry, Alexa," Liana whispered. "Why did I ever leave?"

Up above, Lily barked excitedly. Liana looked up and saw Alexa's necklace dangling from the puppy's neck!

"Alexa's necklace!" Liana exclaimed. "Lydia's magic didn't work when Alexa was *wearing* it!" Liana held her arms up to the puppy and called, "Drop, Lily, drop." Lily bowed her head, and the necklace dropped into Liana's hands. Liana knelt down and slipped it around Alexa's neck.

"Please let this work," she whispered. Then she held her stone in one hand, and grasped Alexa's hand with the other. "Best friends today, tomorrow, and always."

Liana's stone glowed magically . . . and so did Alexa's!

Alexa sat up. "Liana? Where are we?" she asked.

It had worked!

Beaming, Liana quickly explained that Lydia had forced Melody to take her to the Diamond Castle.

Alexa's eyes widened. "We have to stop them!"

Liana grabbed her best friend's hand. "We're going to climb up together," she said bravely. "I'll help you. I won't leave your side."

Alexa nodded, and her eyes suddenly filled with tears. "I'm so sorry, Liana. About everything."

"Me, too," Liana said.

Together, the girls climbed out of the lava pit. Lily was waiting to greet them, wagging her tail and licking their faces.

The girls and Lily hurried out into the dawn, leaving Lydia's gloomy cave behind. They hadn't been walking for long when the sound of hooves echoed through the air. It was Jeremy, Ian . . . and Sparkles! The little puppy had found the girls!

The twins pulled Liana and Alexa up onto their horses.

"You actually think this mad plan will work?" Jeremy asked, once the girls had filled them in.

Liana nodded firmly. "It has to."

Jeremy looked over at Ian. "What do you think?"

Ian shook his head. "Doom. Disaster. Catastrophe."

Jeremy laughed. "So we're in, then?"

"Definitely," Ian responded.

Chapter 11

Meanwhile, Lydia and Melody flew through the air on Slyder's back, toward the Diamond Castle. Melody directed the giant serpent toward the misty glade and a pond nearby.

Slyder glided in for a landing, and Lydia peered around the glade suspiciously. "This can't be it," she scoffed, holding up Melody's mirror. "If you want me to believe that the Diamond Castle is here, give me the key. Or I throw you in the pond, and your friends never come out of the cave."

Melody looked around frantically, her eyes landing on a large boulder. The boulder had a series of holes in it that created a diamond shape.

"The key is . . . the diamond in the diamond," Melody said slowly, pointing to the boulder.

Lydia strode over to the large rock, holding Melody's mirror in one hand.

"Each slot holds a diamond," Melody continued.

Lydia slipped a sparkling diamond bracelet off her arm. She snapped it apart, collecting the individual diamonds in one hand. Lydia placed one diamond after another in the boulder. Eventually, she slotted the final diamond into place.

Nothing happened.

"You've been playing with me!" Lydia cried.

Melody's eyes blazed. "You can't be the only muse, Lydia. It isn't right. The Diamond Castle is meant for everybody."

"Great singers don't need a chorus," Lydia said darkly.

Suddenly, eerie music drifted from the nearby trees. Slyder turned toward it, weaving between the trees, and spotted Ian playing his guitar. Just as Slyder prepared to attack, Jeremy dropped down from the branches overhead, landing on Slyder's back!

Slyder wriggled and bucked, sending Jeremy tumbling. But the twins weren't giving up so easily!

With Slyder distracted, Liana and Alexa

ran toward the glade. Lydia couldn't hide her surprise upon seeing them.

Neither could Melody. "I knew they'd come," she cried.

Lydia pulled out her sinister flute and began to play. Liana and Alexa weren't wearing their necklaces!

Lydia turned to the nearby pond, using her magic to whip the water into a dangerous

whirlpool. "Into the water," she instructed the girls.

The two girls walked toward the water, their eyes glazed over. But just as they passed Lydia, Liana grabbed the flute from her hands and tossed it to Alexa.

They weren't spellbound, after all!

Both girls pulled out their magical necklaces and slipped them around their necks, where they belonged. The necklaces had protected them, even in their pockets.

"Give me the flute!" Lydia raged. She raised Melody's mirror, ready to shatter it against a rock. "My flute, or I break the mirror."

"Don't let her have it!" Melody yelled. She closed her eyes tight, concentrating, and cracked the mirror from the inside.

"Fool!" Lydia cried, tossing the mirror into the pond and turning to Alexa. "Give me the flute."

As Lydia moved toward Alexa to grab the flute, Alexa tossed the instrument to Liana. "Save Melody!" Liana called to Alexa after she caught it.

Alexa rushed to the edge of the pond, just in time to see Sparkles splashing through the water. The little puppy grabbed the edge of Melody's mirror in her teeth. Lily jumped in, too, helping her friend swim desperately to the shore.

Alexa pulled the puppies out of the water and dried the mirror on her skirt. She spun around to see Liana holding Lydia's flute over the swirling whirlpool! Lydia lunged for her magic flute, and the evil muse and her magic instrument plunged into the raging whirlpool.

The water current was too strong for her and Lydia vanished beneath the shadowy water.

Chapter 12

Now released from Lydia's spell, the whirlpool settled back into a peaceful pond. Liana looked out at the water. "I can't believe it," she said quietly.

Alexa nodded. "It's over. Finally over."

The girls carefully lifted Melody's broken mirror and called for their friend. Only their own reflections looked back at them.

At that moment, Jeremy and Ian ran

into the glade. They had beaten Slyder —
for now.

"Where's the Diamond Castle?" Ian
asked.

"I believe it's here," Liana said, looking
out into the glade.

"How can you believe in what you can't
see?" Jeremy wondered aloud.

Liana and Alexa looked at each other.
Jeremy's words had reminded them of the
words to Melody's song. What if the song
was the key? The two girls began to sing,
*"Believe and sing from your heart — you'll see
how your song will hold the key."*

The ground trembled. Music filled the
air. And the incredible Diamond Castle
rose from the glade, sparkling with
diamonds and jewels. Water cascaded from

its fountains, and a bridge jutted across the water.

It was the most beautiful sight any of them had ever seen!

Together, the girls, the twins, and the puppies walked across the bridge. Liana held the cracked mirror in her hand.

As they crossed to the castle, the girls'
dresses magically transformed into
beautiful gowns. A glimmer of magic
enveloped the mirror in Liana's hand,
carrying it away.

And suddenly, Melody stood before
them — free from the mirror at last!

She ran to the girls, squeezing them in
a hug.

The grand hall inside the castle glittered with diamonds. The sun shone through a giant window overhead as Melody led Liana and Alexa up a set of stone steps. "The muses' instruments are up here," she said.

At the top of the stairs, she opened the door to the music room. The magical lyre and lute were perched on a jeweled stone pedestal. Liana and Alexa couldn't help gasping at the sight of them.

"If we play the instruments now . . ." Liana began.

Melody nodded, smiling widely. "The muses will come home."

But to their surprise, Slyder appeared through a tall window! Lydia rode on his back — dripping wet and holding her horrible flute.

Lydia raised her flute and began to play.

With the very first notes lingering in the air, the muses' instruments started to turn to stone!

Liana and Alexa gasped, and immediately grabbed the lyre and lute. The stones on their necklaces were glowing, protecting them — including both instruments.

They began to play the magical instruments and Melody sang the song that she had taught them — the song of the Diamond Castle. Good music battled evil, and the flute was magically lifted from Lydia's hands . . . and both she and Slyder turned to stone.

Jeremy and Ian burst into the room, gaping at the statues of Lydia and Slyder.

Jeremy looked at his twin. "These girls are a tough act to follow," he noted.

❀ ❀ ❀

Thanks to Melody, Liana, Alexa, and their friends, Lydia's horrible magic was undone across the land. Best of all, the muses, Dori and Phedra, returned to the Diamond Castle. They presented Liana and Alexa with beautiful diamond tiaras and appointed them Princesses of Music. They gave Ian and Jeremy electric blue guitars.

Then they turned to Melody, handing her a golden flute.

"This is for you, Melody," Phedra said warmly. "You are no longer an apprentice. You now replace Lydia as the third muse."

Melody was thrilled. She turned to Liana and Alexa. "Will you stay with us?" she asked.

Alexa smiled. "Once I would have said yes in the blink of an eye. But now, I just want my old home back. It was more than enough."

"We thought you might say that," Dori said knowingly. She handed Liana a small rose plant and passed a small violet to Alexa.

Dori and Phedra played a few notes on their magical instruments, and the flowers bloomed in the girls' hands. Inside each one was a perfect sparkling diamond. Liana and Alexa couldn't believe their eyes.

"Is it enough to rebuild your cottage and restore your garden?" Melody asked.

Liana shook her head. "It's too much."

"You gave up everything to help us," Dori reminded them. "Allow us to help you." With that, she led the girls outside, where a beautiful diamond carriage was waiting to take them home.

Conclusion

"I would have hated it if Alexa and Liana didn't stay friends," Stacie said, back in Barbie's bedroom.

Barbie nodded. "Me, too. Best friends stick together." She smiled at Teresa.

Stacie was quiet for a minute. "Do you think Courtney is sorry for what she said?" she asked softly. "I'm sorry for what I said."

"Maybe you should tell her that," Barbie suggested.

Stacie jumped up and gave Barbie a hug before running out of the room.

"Nice job," Teresa said, nudging Barbie with her elbow.

"Timing is everything!" Barbie laughed and picked up her guitar. "Now, where were we?"

Smiling, the two best friends began to sing — together.